BILLY LAZROE
AND THE KING OF THE SEA

A TALE OF THE NORTHWEST

BILLY LAZROE

AND THE KING OF THE SEA

A TALE OF THE NORTHWEST

WRITTEN BY **Eric A. Kimmel**

ILLUSTRATED BY **Michael Steirnagle**

Browndeer Press

Harcourt Brace & Company

San Diego   New York   London

One rainy morning in April 1885, Billy Lazroe was born on a houseboat anchored in the Willamette River, a mile up from Portland, Oregon. Billy's father had been first mate on a clipper ship, and his mother came from a family of seafarers. So it was only natural that Billy Lazroe arrived in the world with salt water in his veins.

Billy's mother sang him to sleep with sea chanteys. His first toy was a ship in a bottle. He learned to read and write by copying the entries his father made in a ship's log. It was no wonder that Billy Lazroe grew up to be a sailor.

Billy went to sea when he was fourteen years old. He was almost twenty before he saw home again. By then he had experienced enough adventures to fill a storybook. He had seen chunks of ice as big as mountains tumble off the glaciers on the Alaskan coast. He had watched gray whales giving birth to their calves in the warm waters of the Gulf of California. He had smelled the spice winds, heavy with the fragrance of cloves and nutmeg, blowing across the Sunda Strait from the island of Java.

He had been capsized, ship-wrecked, becalmed, and run aground. He had known hunger and thirst, sweltering heat and bone-cracking cold. He had fought pirates and cannibals. He had seen his shipmates perish in ways that make the blood run cold to tell of it. Dinny O'Hara's head, smoked and dried, hanging from the eaves of a hut in New Guinea. Charley Boyle, swallowed by a shark off Christmas Island. Sam Moore, blown from the rigging in a typhoon and never seen again. The more Billy saw of death, the more he cherished life, and as much as he loved the sea, he feared the blue-green water that one day would become his grave.

Every sailor loves a good tune, and none could sing a sea chantey better than Billy Lazroe. He'd take out his concertina and sing in a fine, strong voice, "As I was awalking down Paradise Street . . ." or "What shall we do with the drunken sailor. . . ?"

Now strange to say, no matter how calm the ocean might be, a breeze always blew up when Billy started singing. "That's Davy Jones, the King of the Sea, sending fair winds in thanks for the music," Billy's shipmates would whisper. And who could say it wasn't so?

Of all the songs he knew, and he knew dozens, Billy's favorite tune was one he wrote himself. It was about the beautiful Willamette River that flowed by his home in Oregon.

Columbia's broad
and the Umpqua is wild.
Siletz and Nehalem
are sleepy and mild.
But lovely Willamette
will always be true.
I'll always come home,
sweet Willamette, to you.

One spring, after three years at sea, Billy came home to Oregon. In all that time he'd missed nothing so much as the taste of fresh-baked Northwest salmon. So one evening at dusk, when the salmon were running, Billy took his concertina and fishing pole and went down to the riverbank. He sat himself down on an old log and cast his line into the water. The lights of Portland shined above the trees. Shoals of stars glimmered overhead as the salmon leaped. By the light of the moon he saw their silver bodies glide beneath the water.

Constellations rose and set in the sky as Billy waited in vain for the salmon to bite. Discouraged, he rested his fishing pole against the log, took up the squeeze-box, and began to play.

Hardly had Billy fingered the first notes when the river began to bubble and boil like a kettle of chowder. The water parted and an enormous figure rose from the depths. It spoke with a voice like distant thunder.

"Ahoy, Billy Lazroe! Do you know me?"

"Davy Jones, the King of the Sea!" Billy gasped. "What are you doing in the Willamette River?"

"I love your music, Billy. I've come to invite you to play for my shipmates down in Davy Jones's locker."

Billy wasn't eager for an invitation like that. Sailors who pass through the swinging doors of Davy Jones's locker never return.

"I'd love to, Davy," Billy replied. "But this squeeze-box needs mending. Can't it wait for another day?"

"I'll wait, Billy. I'll even pay in advance, to seal the bargain. But don't delay too long," said Davy Jones, and he disappeared beneath the water.

Moonlight shimmered on the quiet face of the river. Billy Lazroe took up his fishing pole again. It was only a dream, he told himself. Suddenly he felt a tug on his line. He had hooked a canvas sack. Inside was a handful of lustrous pearls.

The next morning Billy borrowed a skiff and rowed down to Portland. As he strolled along the waterfront, he came upon the finest ship he had ever seen. Her sails were whiter than the snows of Mount Hood and her graceful figurehead as charming as the waiter girls at Erickson's Saloon.

"She's a fine ship. I wish she were mine," Billy told the captain.

"What's her name?"

"*Willamette.* And she's for sale."

"Will you take this for her?" Billy showed the captain the pearls in his pocket.

"Those pearls could buy a fleet!" the captain said.

"I only want one ship," Billy replied. "This one."

That's how Billy Lazroe became captain of the *Willamette*. And on clear nights when the moon hung above the mainmast and the Milky Way filled with stars like the salmon swimming upstream, he would take out his concertina and sing.

But lovely Willamette
will always be true.
I'll always come home,
sweet Willamette, to you.

As he sang, the breeze came up to fill the sails. The sailors on deck overheard their captain whisper, "One more day, Davy. Give me one more day and I'll come to you, just as I promised."

Seven years passed.

One August night on the South China Sea, the ocean began to bubble like a kettle of chowder. As the terrified sailors watched, a giant figure arose from the deep. Davy Jones pointed his finger at Billy Lazroe.

"My shipmates are waiting," Davy Jones thundered.

"I'll come tomorrow. I promise," said Billy Lazroe.

"You're coming now!" said Davy Jones.

Billy bade his crew farewell. With his concertina tucked beneath his arm, he leaped into the ocean.

Down, down, down sank Billy
Lazroe through the blue-green
water until he arrived at the bottom
of the sea.

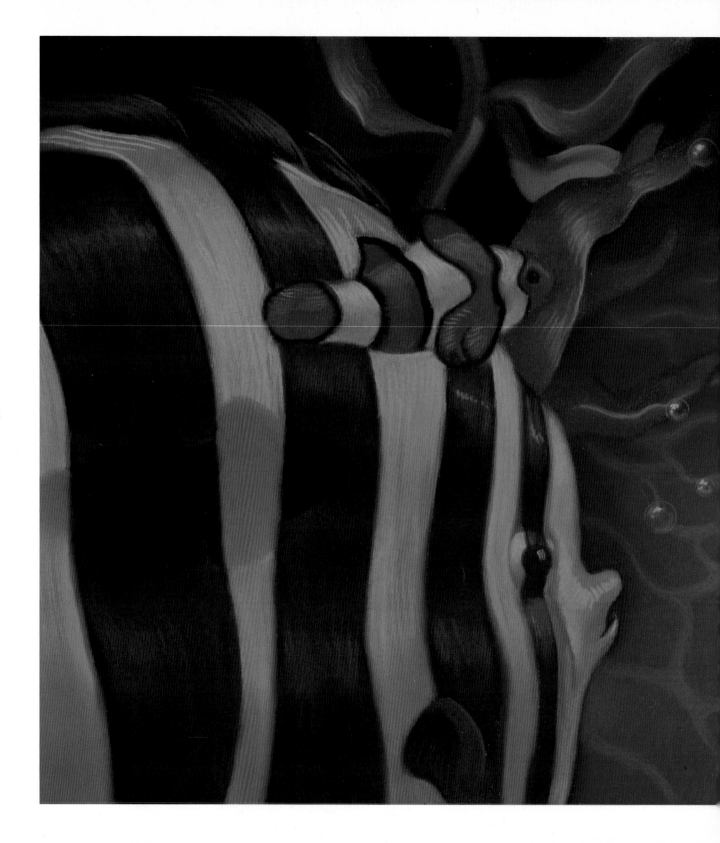

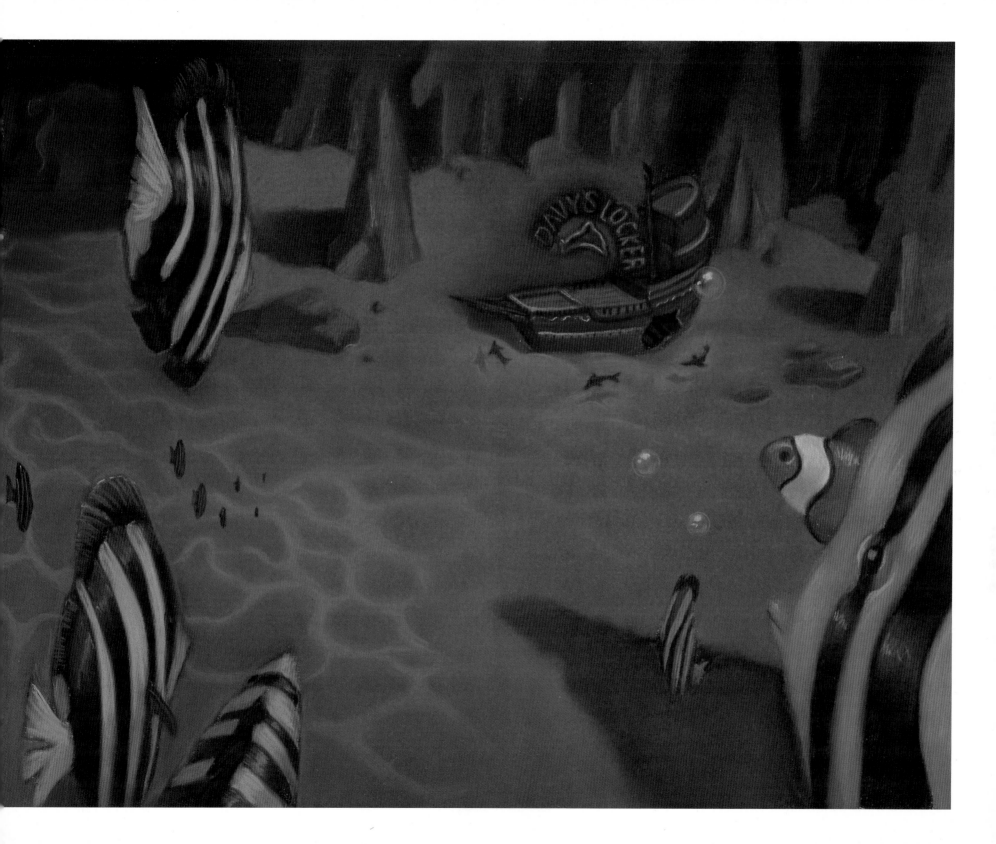

He walked through the swinging doors of Davy Jones's locker.
Seafaring men of every age and
from every country filled the room.
Billy recognized some of his friends
and called to them.

"Ahoy, Dinny! I'm glad you got
your head back. I'll bet you gave
that shark a bellyache, Charley.
Sam! So this is where the wind
blew you."

They didn't answer.

"Can't they see me?" Billy
asked Davy Jones.

"They can't see you because
you're still alive. Only dead sailors
live here. But they'll hear you if
you play for them. Play for my
shipmates, Billy, and for all the
brave sailors who have gone to
their rest at the bottom of the sea."

Billy Lazroe took up his concertina and began to play. He began with a merry hornpipe and the rollicking chanteys that sailors love. After a time the music grew sad as Billy thought of home. He sang of the Oregon country and the quiet Willamette River. The notes echoed the cry of a heron among the reeds, the slap of a fish's tail, the soft scraping of a canoe passing through the shallows, the murmur of wind-blown reeds, the drift of mist against moss-covered rocks. He sang of all the things he loved most, which he might never see again.

The sailors began singing together—Malay fishermen, Chinese boatmen, New England whalers, Polynesian voyagers; the crews of a thousand vessels lost in the blue-green depths of the sea. Their voices filled with the shriek of the wind, the gulls' cry, the rush of spray bursting over a rock, and the lonely voice of a whale singing in the depths of perpetual night.

When the last note died away, Davy Jones said, "That was worth the wait, Billy. You should have come sooner. One of my daughters heard you singing one summer night and fell in love with you. You've made her pine for seven years. That was cruel, Billy, but she forgives you. If you can pick her out from all the rest, I'll let her go with you to the world above."

Davy Jones clapped his hands. His daughters, all the rivers of the world, came into the hall. They were as beautiful as stars, and they all looked alike, except for one who wore a single pearl around her neck. The pearl reminded Billy of the full moon shining on the Willamette River.

"You are the one," Billy Lazroe said. "Tell me your name."

She replied, "You know it already. My name is Willamette."

Billy took her by the hand. The lights of Davy Jones's locker began to fade.

"Hold fast to your bride, Billy," Davy Jones called. "Keep your eyes straight ahead. Don't turn around till you reach home port."

Billy rose from the bottom of the ocean, clutching Willamette's hand as tightly as a shipwrecked sailor clings to a floating log. He drifted up through schools of squid and strange shining creatures that have no names. An octopus brushed him with its tentacles. A porpoise swam alongside him. The water turned light green as he rose higher. Billy looked up toward the rays of sunlight piercing the depths.

A shark lunged past Billy. He turned around to protect his bride— but it was too late. Willamette was gone.

The morning sun found Billy Lazroe lying beside the river. His squeeze-box lay next to him, wrapped in seaweed. Clutched in his hand was a luminous pearl, as bright as the moon.

The tale ends here. Billy Lazroe told his story the next evening to Georgie Taylor and the others at Erickson's Saloon. Jim Oren, the piano player, claims to have seen the pearl. Then Billy walked out the door into the night, and that was the last time anyone saw him.

Nobody knows what happened to Billy Lazroe. Some say he sailed north to the Yukon to look for gold. Others say he was lost in a storm off the coast of China. Or somewhere in the Philippines. Or maybe Samoa.

Then there are those who say Billy never went anywhere. He just kept walking, straight out the door and into the river to join his bride down in Davy Jones's locker.

Now on stormy nights on the Oregon coast, when the wind howls and the sea hurls itself against the cliffs, sailors say it's Billy Lazroe, singing for Davy Jones and his shipmates, and the beautiful river he loves best.

Columbia's broad
and the Umpqua is wild.
Siletz and Nehalem
are sleepy and mild.
But lovely Willamette
will always be true.
I'll always come home,
sweet Willamette, to you.

Kimmel, Eric A.
Billy Lazroe and the King of the Sea: a tale of the Northwest/
Eric A. Kimmel; illustrated by Michael Steirnagle.
p. cm.
"Browndeer Press."
Summary: Billy Lazroe, a sailor from Oregon, jumps into the
ocean at the command of Davy Jones and falls in love
with one of Davy's daughters.
ISBN 0-15-200108-5
[1. Folklore—Oregon.] I. Steirnagle, Michael, ill. II. Title.
PZ8.1.K567Bi 1996
398.2—dc20
[E] 95-11715

First edition
A C E F D B

The illustrations in this book were done in pastels
on Stonehenge paper.
The display type was set in Rio Grande.
The text type was set in Cochin.
Color separations by Bright Arts, Ltd., Singapore
Printed and bound by Tien Wah Press, Singapore
This book was printed with soya-based inks on Leykam recycled
paper, which contains more than 20 percent postconsumer waste
and has a total recycled content of at least 50 percent.
Production supervision by Warren Wallerstein and Pascha Gerlinger
Designed by Lydia D'moch

*To Judy Olinger, teacher and friend,
who brought the gift of reading
to the children of Oregon*

—E. A. K.

For my wife, Adele

—M. S.

AUTHOR'S NOTE

Billy Lazroe and the King of the Sea was conceived
as a Northwest American version of the old
Russian tale *Sadko, the Merchant of Novgorod*.
Oregonians have the same ongoing love affair
with the Willamette River as the citizens of
Novgorod had with the Volkhov.

Erickson's Saloon was a turn-of-the-century
Portland landmark, a gathering place for sailors,
loggers, and thrill-seekers from all over the
Northwest. The establishment fell on hard times
with the coming of Prohibition, when John
Erickson, the proprietor, was arrested for
bootlegging. He died in poverty, but his building
still stands in Portland's Old Town, not far from
the banks of the Willamette River.